Shivers™

CAMP FEAR

M. D. Spenser

Paradise Press, Inc.

Plantation, Florida

Published by Paradise Press, Inc. by arrangement with River Publishing, Inc. All
right, title and interest to the "SHIVERS" logo and design are owned by River
Publishing, Inc. No portion of the "SHIVERS" logo and design may be reproduced
in part or whole without prior written permission from River Publishing, Inc. An
application for a registered trademark of the "SHIVERS" logo and design is pend-
ing with the Federal Patent and Trademark office.

ISBN 1-57657-144-0

EXCLUSIVE DISTRIBUTION BY PARADISE PRESS, INC.

Cover Illustration by Eddie Roseboom

Printed in the U.S.A.

30780

To Lindsay Jane

Chapter One

Jane unzipped her backpack and checked its contents one last time.

Sleeping bag? Check.

Sweatshirt? Check.

Extra jeans and T-shirts? Check.

Flashlight, canteen, bug spray? Check.

Clean underwear, socks, toothbrush? Check.

She couldn't be more ready. She had packed for this overnight trip days ago, but she was full of nervous energy. Checking her stuff helped relax her.

The entire sixth grade class at Laurel Acres Elementary School was going on a three-day trip to the mountains. Jane was totally psyched.

She had only been camping once, when she was three, but she didn't remember it at all. Her mom had said the whole trip was better forgotten. And that had seemed to end her family's camping days.

Now she was getting to go camping with her best friend Lindsay, and all their other school friends, for three days and two nights!

Jane wasn't sure if this counted as real camping. After all, they were going to sleep in cabins. But there were no hot showers and no flush toilets. To Jane, that sounded an awful lot like roughing it.

Lindsay's family went camping all the time. She made it sound like the best time in the world.

Well, we shall soon see, Jane thought. She threw her backpack over her shoulder and ran downstairs to eat the last home-cooked meal she'd have for three whole days.

When she reached the kitchen, she found her mom just as charged up as she was.

"Now remember, honey," her mom said, "always stay with your assigned group. Don't go wandering off with Lindsay and get lost. I don't want to get a call that something happened to you, or hear that you caused the teachers any trouble."

Jane rolled her eyes. Her mother was quite a

worrier.

"Relax, Mom," she said. "I'll be fine. You know I never give Miss Farlie a hard time."

"I also know that you and Lindsay often have your heads in the clouds," her mom said.

Now, *that* was true. Jane couldn't deny it.

Sometimes, when she and Lindsay were together, the rest of the world seemed to disappear. Time flew by. The next thing they knew, they were late for an important event. Sometimes they forgot their responsibilities completely.

They just enjoyed being with each other so much that nothing else mattered. They seemed to read each other's minds. Often, one would finish a sentence the other had started. Jane had read a book about twins who could do that.

She and Lindsay were close in age, but they weren't twins. They weren't even sisters.

Although, to Jane, it felt as if they were. Perhaps that was because she had no brothers or sisters of her own. She and Lindsay had been friends since preschool, and she figured Lindsay was the closest thing to a sister she would ever have.

Not that they were the same as each other. They weren't. Jane tended to be more cautious. Lindsay, maybe because of all her experience camping in the woods, was braver. It was as if they were two halves of the same puzzle, each supplying something the other was missing.

Lindsay had two brothers, but she loved Jane like a sister, too. She told Jane that she wished she didn't have any brothers.

Everybody always wants what they don't have, Jane thought.

She heard a honk and raced out the door without even touching her breakfast.

"Mom, Lindsay's here to drive me," she shouted.

"Gotta go! Bye!" She gave her mother a kiss and flew out the door.

Chapter Two

The school yard bustled with excitement.

There were three sixth grade classes at Laurel Acres. Altogether, sixty-five kids were going on the camping trip.

Lindsay and Jane said a hurried good-bye to Lindsay's mom and dashed off to join their group.

Miss Farlie was a really cool teacher. She put friends with friends whenever she could. She separated troublemakers from each other, but Jane and her friends, who didn't cause much trouble, usually got to take trips together.

Jane expected to be grouped with Lindsay, Carolyn, Jaimie, Alyssa and Katie. The six of them had been friends for a long time, and Miss Farlie knew it.

But they were in for a surprise.

Jane got her hands on a group list and couldn't

believe her eyes. Listed under Cabin 8 were her name and Lindsay's — but bunking with them would be two girls she would never want to sit next to in class, let alone sleep next to in a cabin!

Chelsea Daniels and Molly Clark. What a pair!

Chelsea was the snootiest girl in town. She was stuck up and mean, too.

Molly was a total nerd, a real loser. Jane felt bad for her, but she also thought that, in her own weird way, Molly enjoyed her nerd status.

What a field day Chelsea will have picking on Molly, Jane thought.

Attendance was taken, and then all sixty-five kids piled onto two huge buses and headed for Camp Armonk.

Camp Armonk had once been the summer home of a millionaire and his wife. They'd never had children of their own, and, according to the story Jane had heard, they'd been upset that no children ever enjoyed the beauty of the land, which covered five hundred acres in the mountains.

So, when they died, they left the land to the

state for a camp for kids.

Jane looked out the window as the bus rolled down the highway. Her class had raised money for this all year. She couldn't believe they were finally on their way.

Each group of kids was required to do a research project at Camp Armonk. Jane and Lindsay had been learning about geology in school, and they planned to search for rock and mineral specimens.

Maybe, Jane thought, they would find some diamonds or some gold!

After a couple of hours, the bus turned off the main road onto what looked like a trail. Jane couldn't believe these huge buses could fit on this narrow track in the woods. The road, if you could call it that, was made only of dirt, and it was very bumpy.

The bus jounced and creaked. Jane bounced in her seat. Her knees banged into the back of the seat in front of her.

Tall trees formed a canopy over the road. It felt as if the buses were driving through a long green tunnel.

After a couple of miles, they stopped in a clearing. Out the window, Jane saw the most rundown cabins she had ever seen in her life.

Everyone piled off the buses and gathered for instructions. One of the teachers told them to go to their cabins, unpack, and meet back at the flagpole in half an hour.

Jane and Lindsay ran off to find Cabin 8 as fast as they could, so they could get beds next to each other.

The cabins were in numerical order. The girls had been assigned to cabins one through eight, on the right side of the flagpole. The boys were in cabins nine through sixteen, on the left.

Jane and Lindsay ran down the row of cabins. As they approached Cabin 8, they realized they would be sleeping in the last cabin in line — right at the edge of the woods, which loomed, dark and ominous, next to the cabin.

They looked at each other. Without speaking, Jane knew that Lindsay was thinking the same thing she was. This might get creepy.

They pushed the cabin door open and were surprised to find Chelsea inside. She had already tested all the cots and claimed the least lumpy one for herself.

Jane and Lindsay chose the two beds at the back, and began unpacking.

As she took her stuff out of her backpack, Jane gave herself an invisible pat on the back for having followed Miss Farlie's packing list to the letter. She glanced at Lindsay's stuff and saw that Lindsay had done the same.

Chelsea, however, was another story.

From her oversized duffel bag she removed a portable CD player, a blow dryer, a hand-held video game, four sweaters, three pairs of shoes, hair spray, perfume, a pillow in a satin case, and a ton of other stuff that was not on Miss Farlie's list.

Jane wondered whether Chelsea had brought anything that *was* on the list.

"Chelsea, didn't you bring a flashlight and a canteen?" Lindsay asked.

"Listen creeps," Chelsea snapped. "What I packed is none of your business. For that matter, what

I *do* is none of your business. So why don't you two Camp Fire Girls just keep to your own side of the cabin?"

Jane looked at Lindsay and raised her eyebrows. Oh, boy, Jane thought. We're in for three days of torture. She could tell, from the way Lindsay's eyebrows shot up, too, that she was thinking the exact same thing.

A loud thump interrupted her thoughts. Then she heard another thump.

Jane and Lindsay looked at each other and froze.

"Wh-wh-what was th-that?" Chelsea stuttered. She was nasty, Jane thought, but she was clearly not brave.

The thumps stopped. They stood in silence.

Nobody moved. The only sound Jane heard was her own nervous breathing.

Then she heard a scratching sound as if something was slithering over the ground outside the cabin door.

The sound grew louder. And louder still.

Slowly, creaking eerily on its hinges, the door to the cabin began to swing open.

Chapter Three

The three girls gasped and jumped back in fear.

The door, creaking louder, continued to swing open. Jane put her hands to her lips. She felt her eyes bulging out of her head. She wanted to scream, but her throat felt so tight that no sound came out.

She looked at Lindsay and Chelsea. They watched in silent horror as well.

Suddenly, the door swung all the way open.

Jane yelped in fear.

Then she heaved a huge sigh of relief. In through the door, on her hands and knees, crawled Molly.

"What the heck are you *doing* down there, dork?" Chelsea shouted. "You scared me half to death!"

"Sorry," Molly replied meekly. "I stumbled on

something and dropped my stuff. My glasses fell off. I can't see too well without them."

"Next time look where you're going, lame-brain," Chelsea said. Angrily, she turned her back and went back to her unpacking.

"Come on, Molly," Jane said. "We'll help you find your glasses."

She and Lindsay led Molly outside and began searching for her glasses.

Jane stood outside the cabin and looked around. She had run to the cabin so quickly, trying to get a bed next to Lindsay, that she hadn't even noticed her surroundings.

Camp Armonk was beautiful. Evergreen trees rose high into the sky. The smaller trees had the un-mistakable look of spring, with light green leaves sprouting and unfolding against the dark branches.

Sunlight filtered through the trees, casting pools of light and shadow across the ground. It made it hard to find Molly's glasses — even if you had good eyesight.

Jane noticed that the cabin was slightly elevated, set up off the ground a bit. She wondered whether the glasses had fallen under the front steps.

She got down on her hands and knees to look. It was too dark to see anything, and the space between the cabin and the ground was narrow.

Then she remembered her flashlight.

"Be right back," she shouted.

She darted into the cabin and grabbed her flashlight off the cot. Thank goodness she was prepared.

"Where's the fire?" snarled Chelsea.

Jane ignored this remark and flew back out of the cabin. She crawled on her stomach until half of her body was under the cabin. She flipped on the flashlight. A narrow beam of light shone a few feet ahead of her.

As she peered into the darkness, she heard a slithering sound, just like the one she had heard before.

But that had been Molly feeling around for her glasses, Jane thought. Now, Molly and Lindsay were in the clearing, so they couldn't be making this noise.

A lump formed in Jane's throat.

She heard the noise again.

There was only one thing that could make a slithering sound like that.

A snake.

If there were snakes under her cabin, she thought, she was sleeping on the bus. Snakes were one thing Jane really feared.

Not that they were the only thing she was afraid of. She was a little timid, she knew, and not an experienced camper. There was a whole list of things she was afraid of. But snakes topped the list. They were number one. She could not stand them.

The slithering noise continued now without stopping. It sounded like it was approaching, getting nearer and nearer and nearer.

"I'm outta here!" Jane said aloud. She began to slide backwards, frantically trying to wriggle out from under the cabin.

As she moved, her flashlight beam jumped around. She thought she saw a glimmer of light just out of her reach.

That must be Molly's glasses, she thought.

She knew she had to grab them, but the slithering sounded really close now.

She held her breath, swallowed hard, and slid forward, stretching her arm out until it felt like it would pop out of its socket.

"Got 'em," she said.

With the glasses in her hand, she tried to retreat from the darkness. The slithering sounded so close she could barely breathe. She tried to move back but she couldn't budge.

A shiver ran down her spine.

The belt loop from her jeans had snagged on a nail that poked out from the cabin floor.

She was stuck!

Chapter Four

"Lindsay! Get me out of here!" Jane screamed.

For a horrible minute, she heard nothing but the slithering. No one had heard her. No one was coming to help. Maybe they had heard the panic in her voice and run the other way.

Then Jane felt hands on her back, unhooking her belt loop from the nail, then pulling on her legs and dragging her from under the cabin. She sat stunned for a minute, blinking in the light.

"Why so panicky, Jane?" Lindsay asked.

Jane looked at her friend with gratitude. She should have known Lindsay the Brave would never let her down, no matter how scared she sounded.

"There's a snake under the cabin." she sputtered. "Maybe millions of them."

"Well, they're probably harmless," Lindsay said. "Did you find Molly's glasses?"

Molly, her eyes bulging as she tried to see, walked slowly toward the cabin to find out what the commotion was.

Jane held out the glasses.

"Here they are Molly," she said. "And by the way, you owe me a *big* one."

Meek as ever, Molly thanked Jane and went back inside. Jane and Lindsay followed — and they could not believe what they saw.

Chelsea was crouched on the floor, laughing hysterically.

"What's so funny?" Lindsay asked.

It didn't take the girls long to see the twisted wire hanger dangling from Chelsea's hand.

"I found a crack in the floor and poked one of my hangers through," Chelsea said. "You guys are so pathetically gullible."

Chelsea tossed the hanger on the bed and ran out of the cabin laughing.

Suddenly, Jane understood there had been no

snakes. Only Chelsea, a wire hanger, and her mean sense of humor.

These were going to be three *very* long days.

It was nearly time to meet back at the flagpole so Jane and Lindsay helped Molly unpack. She might be a nerd, but they were stuck with her for the next three days.

Might as well make the best of it, Jane figured. If they convinced Molly to side with them, they would outnumber Chelsea.

When Molly's stuff was put away, the three girls raced to the flagpole.

Miss Farlie handed each group a compass and a map of the campgrounds.

"Take good care of these," she said. "There is no copy machine up here so if you lose your map, you're out of luck."

Chelsea marched up and grabbed the stuff for Cabin 8.

"I'll take those Miss Farlie," she said. "I'm the only one in my group who even thought to bring a fanny pack. The map and compass will be safe with me."

"Too bad she won't have a clue how to use them," Lindsay whispered to Jane.

"OK, everybody gather around," Miss Farlie shouted.

Hardly anyone heard her. She could have used a megaphone. The kids were pretty loud.

Finally everyone settled down and gathered in a big group around her.

"These woods here are relatively safe, but that doesn't mean you should be careless," Miss Farlie said. "Never leave the cabin area on your own. Keep your map with you at all times. If you are going hiking, carry water and your compass. Please take some time to familiarize yourself with the map. There are some areas that are off limits to you."

She looked around to make sure that everyone was paying attention. Some of the kids were studying their maps. Others were turning their compasses this way and that, watching how the needles always pointed the same way.

Miss Farlie clapped to get everyone's attention.

"Meals will be prepared here in the flagpole area," she said. "Breakfast is at 8:30 sharp; lunch will be at 12:30; and dinner is served at 6 o'clock. Everybody *must* check in at every meal. There's a work roster posted on the tree at the back of the clearing. Please check it so you'll know which meal your cabin is supposed to help with."

Off in the crowd, Jane heard Chelsea whining to her friends.

"I can't believe she expects us to work!" Chelsea moaned. "This is like boot camp."

"Did you have something you wanted to share with the group Miss Daniels?" Miss Farlie asked.

Miss Farlie always called you miss or mister when she didn't like the way you were acting.

"I was just saying how nice this camp is, Miss Farlie," Chelsea said. The other girls giggled. Miss Farlie glared at her.

"Most of you already know what you're researching while you are here," Miss Farlie continued. "But those of you who never came up with your own project idea — and you know who you are — have been paired with a team that did come prepared.

"As you know, your projects will be graded when we return to school. Those of you who did not prepare a project in advance will receive a grade one point below your team's final grade."

Jane and Lindsay smiled at each other. After all, they had worked hard on their geology research. Why should Molly and Chelsea get credit for that when they hadn't done a thing?

Jane heard Chelsea's voice hissing in her ear.

"You bookworms better have come up with something easy to do in this wretched wilderness," Chelsea spat. "I have no intention of traipsing around the woods for three days getting all sweaty."

"Doesn't look like you have much choice, Miss Daniels," Lindsay replied.

She and Jane looked at each other and giggled at the thought of Chelsea worrying about her hair while they dug for minerals.

At school, Jane and Lindsay avoided Chelsea. She acted as if she ran the place.

At Camp Armonk, it was a different story. She didn't run the place, Jane thought. She had to work on their project. And she had no idea what she was doing in the woods.

And even though Jane was not an experienced camper, Lindsay was.

For once Jane thought she and Lindsay might have the upper hand.

Chapter Five

It was 12:30 by the time Miss Farlie finished giving all her instructions.

All the kids pushed their way onto the buses to grab the lunches they had brought from home. Off the bus, they broke into small groups of friends and found spots to picnic.

Lindsay and Jane hooked up with Alyssa, Katie, Jaimie and Carolyn. As they ate lunch, they compared notes and realized that none of them had faired very well in the cabin-mate department.

Alyssa and Katie shared a cabin with a troublemaker named Angela and a jock named Kim. Jaimie and Carolyn roomed with Janet, one of Chelsea's snobby friends, and Nancy, a prissy type whose favorite outdoor activity was sun-bathing.

If only the six of them could have been together, it would have been great.

They had all been friends since preschool, except for Jaimie, who had moved to Laurel Acres in third grade. In fourth grade they had started having sleep-over birthday parties.

Katie had a sleep-over party a few weeks ago. They had all stayed up half the night making plans for this camping trip. They had never even considered the possibility that Miss Farlie would separate them.

The mountain air had given them huge appetites. They devoured their lunches.

Jane and Lindsay were anxious to start their project. They made plans to meet their friends again before dinner, then ran off to check the work roster.

Cabins 8 and 16 were assigned to help with tomorrow night's dinner. It would be the last night of the trip, though they would stay through the next day, and the teachers had planned a big barbecue.

The kids were to report for work by 5:30 in the afternoon.

Next, Jane and Lindsay went to look for Molly and Chelsea so they could begin exploring.

They found Molly eating alone under a shady tree. Didn't she have any friends, Jane wondered. Did she eat by herself in the cafeteria at school every day?

Jane couldn't explain why, but seeing Molly alone made her feel guilty.

She had never done anything mean to Molly. She had never teased her, the way Chelsea's group did.

Then again, Jane realized, she had never gone out of her way to be nice to Molly either.

Jane looked at Lindsay. Silently, communicating only with their eyes, they agreed to make Molly feel included.

"Hey, Molly! Finished eating yet?" Jane called, trying to sound cheery.

"I guess so," Molly mumbled.

They heard laughter coming from behind a group of trees and recognized the voices of Chelsea and her friends.

"Come on," Lindsay began. "Let's get this over with."

The three of them tiptoed around the trees and

found Chelsea and Janet in the middle of a circle of kids, holding the wire hanger in her hand and re-enacting the fake snake scare.

Janet was pretending to have lost her glasses. She stumbled around and bumped into things.

Chelsea was shrieking "Snakes! Snakes! Snakes!"

The other kids laughed and hooted. They did not notice Jane, Lindsay and Molly approaching.

Jane was embarrassed, but she realized lots of kids were scared of snakes. She could deal with it.

But she glanced sideways at Molly, and saw she was fighting back tears. Being ignored by Chelsea and her friends was one thing. Being teased by them was another.

Then Jane got a brilliant idea.

She signaled to Lindsay and Molly to hang back. Quietly, they crept to the far side of the trees. The bushes were thicker there. The girls were completely hidden.

Jane found some pebbles. She began tossing them into the trees, aiming just beyond Chelsea and her friends. Lindsay and Molly caught on and began tossing pebbles, too.

"Hey, Chelsea, keep it down," Janet hissed. "Did you guys hear that?"

A hush fell over the group. As each pebble hit the bushes, it made a rustling noise. The girls and boys drew closer to each other. Almost involuntarily, they formed a circle, with their backs together and their faces toward the woods.

Their eyes grew wide with fear.

Jane and her friends had to strain to keep from laughing. Chelsea's gang looked really spooked.

Jane ran out of pebbles. She spotted a few more a couple of steps away. As she started towards them, a twig snapped loudly under her foot.

Chelsea screamed. She and her friends scrambled to their feet and ran back to the flagpole, yelling all the way.

Jane, Molly and Lindsay sat on the ground and held their sides and laughed. It felt good to pay Chelsea back. Nobody had been hurt. There had been no harm done.

It was just a good, old-fashioned practical joke.

Chapter Six

"Gee, Chelsea, you look like you've seen a ghost," Lindsay said.

She, Jane and Molly had joined Chelsea and the others at the flagpole. Jane looked at Lindsay in a way that said you really shouldn't tease her any more. Lindsay rolled her eyes at Jane in a way that said I can't help myself.

The two of them smiled at each other, and almost started laughing again.

"Buzz off, creep," Chelsea snapped.

"I'd love to," Lindsay said. "But our group is starting on the project and, unfortunately, our group includes you."

The four of them headed back to Cabin 8. There, they filled up their canteens — except for Chelsea, of course, who had brought a CD player but not a canteen.

Jane got the map from Chelsea and looked it over.

Two streams ran through the camp, and both flowed into a small lake. It was still early spring, so Jane was sure swimming was out of the question. The water would be too cold.

Besides, they were here to find precious stones and minerals, not to swim.

The map also showed a cliff half a mile down a trail that started right behind their cabin. Further down the trail, past the cliff, a little icon on the map indicated a mine.

It was marked: OFF LIMITS.

Too bad, Jane thought. I bet we could find some great specimens in there.

Lots of other trails zigzagged around the campgrounds. They were all clearly marked and color-coded. Jane was an inexperienced camper, but she figured you'd have to be pretty lame to get lost around here.

She showed the map to the others.

"What do you say we head for the cliff and see what we find?" she said. "It looks like it's pretty close, and we only have a few hours till dinner."

Chelsea grumbled about having to go anyplace at all. The trail would probably wreck her shoes, she said. But she agreed to go.

Molly shrugged. She would agree to anything, Jane thought.

The four of them headed down a broad trail marked with red trail blazes. Lindsay and Jane walked together. Chelsea marched angrily behind them. Molly brought up the rear.

It was a beautiful, warm afternoon. For the first time, Jane began to enjoy her surroundings.

The trees swayed in the breeze, and sunlight dappled their path. Squirrels and chipmunks chattered in the branches. Birds fluttered here and there, building nests or carrying worms to their young.

Also flying around, unfortunately, were bugs. Lots of them.

"Do any of you Girl Scouts have anything useful, like bug spray?" Chelsea moaned. "I'm getting eaten alive."

The bugs swarmed everywhere, but their main target was Chelsea. Jane saw them flying around Chelsea in a great black cloud.

"You didn't put on any of your stupid perfume, did you?" she asked. "Even I know you can't wear perfume when you go hiking!"

"Well, thanks for the tip but what do I do now?" Chelsea said.

The bugs swarmed about her more thickly now. She swatted one arm and then the other. She slapped her cheeks. She started jumping all over the trail, slapping and hopping and swatting and scratching.

Jane tried not to laugh. It wasn't easy.

Then Molly spoke in her usual hushed tones.

"Maybe you could wash off the perfume smell," she said.

"What did Miss Mousy say?" Chelsea snapped, slapping the back of her neck.

"If we wet my bandanna," Molly said, "she could wipe off some of the perfume. It might help."

Jane wasn't sure why Molly cared about helping Chelsea, especially after the way Chelsea had teased her. Maybe Molly wasn't such a nerd after all. Maybe under her awkward facade she was a nice person, just terribly shy.

Molly poured water from her canteen over her bandanna. Chelsea wrenched the bandanna out of her hand and scrubbed her neck and arms until the skin turned red. Then she flung the bandanna back at Molly.

She muttered, "Thanks."

The group resumed the hike. In a few minutes the trail turned sharply.

When the girls rounded the bend, they found themselves perched on the top of a very steep, very high cliff.

Chapter Seven

"This is so cool!" Lindsay said. They were up so high up they could see for miles.

Jane enjoyed the view, too. Until she happened to look down.

Below her, the cliff tumbled about forty feet down to a trail. She saw a red trail blaze nailed to a tree below.

"Hey, dimwits," Chelsea said. "Aren't we supposed to be on the red trail? How the heck did we end up way up here?"

Lindsay and Jane exchanged a look. How had it happened? They had led the way the whole time, and they had been careful to follow the blazes.

They must have gotten distracted and missed a turn, Jane decided. There seemed no way to go forward, and climbing down the face of the cliff looked treacherous.

"I guess we'll have to turn back," Lindsay said.

"Wait," Jane said, "As long as we're up here, let's look around for some specimens. I can get a little farther out over here. I think I see something shining in the stone."

She inched her way along the cliff and scrambled over a boulder. When she dropped down on the other side of the big rock, she could no longer see her friends.

But that was OK. She had been nervous because she had no camping experience, but she was starting to feel braver. The woods weren't so scary after all. They had missed their turn, but big deal. All they had to do was retrace their steps. They were perfectly safe.

She turned her eyes ahead of her to look for specimens.

Then she saw them.

They slithered and writhed in a horrible seething mass, their forked tongues darting in and out.

Snakes!

Her heart froze. She feared nothing in the world more than snakes, and before her in a great pulsing pile writhed a dozen or more. These were no coat hangers. This was no trick.

These were real.

She tried to scream but she could not catch her breath. It felt as if iron bands were tightening around her chest. She couldn't breathe in.

The snakes uncoiled and unraveled themselves and slithered toward her. One opened its mouth, flicking its tongue. Jane saw the two small fangs curving down from the upper jaw.

Closer they slid, and closer.

Jane screamed.

The snakes had nearly reached her feet. Jane stood on tiptoe, wanting to clamber back over the boulder but afraid to turn around.

Why had no one answered her scream? Had they turned back without her, leaving her alone to face a seething mass of snakes by herself?

She screamed again, a long, loud piercing scream of panic.

"LINDSAY!!!"

The words echoed through the forest, bouncing back against the rocky face of the cliff again and again: *"Lindsay... Lindsay... Lindsay."*

The echo died away and the silence of the forest returned. Jane pressed herself flat against the rock, and stretched her arms out from her sides trying to hold onto the hard surface.

From around the boulder, she felt something touch her hand. She screamed and drew back.

"Jane! Are you OK?" It was Lindsay, reaching around the boulder to help her.

Jane felt all the air rush out of her.

"It's OK, Jane," Lindsay said in a reassuring voice. "They won't hurt you. Those snakes are harmless. Just take my hand, OK?"

Slowly, Jane reached out to grab Lindsay's hand — the hand she had drawn away from a moment before. They clasped hands tightly.

Suddenly, Jane could breathe again. Knowing her friend was there allowed her to move. With Lindsay's help, she stepped warily over the writhing creatures. She fell into Lindsay's arms.

"Get me out of here!" she gasped.

The two of them clambered around the crag to safety.

They found Molly crouched on the ground, staring at her watch.

"I was just about to go back for help," Molly said. "I'm glad you're OK, Jane."

"I'm fine." Jane replied, breathing deeply to calm herself. "And only slightly embarrassed. Where's Chelsea? I'm sure she'll have another field day at my expense."

"I doubt it," Lindsay said. "When she heard you scream, she took off with her tail between her legs!"

The three girls laughed just thinking about that. Then they started back down the trail.

Chapter Eight

Back on the trail, Jane felt much better. Walking in the dappled light of the forest, with Lindsay on one side of her and Molly on the other, she felt safe again.

As they walked back to camp, she wondered how they had ended up on that cliff. The map had shown the red trail running along the bottom of the cliff, where they had seen the red blaze.

Where had they taken a wrong turn?

"Let's keep our eyes out for the right trail, so we can find it next time," she said.

"I might not have great eyesight," Molly said, "but I'm pretty sure there were no turns off the main trail. We went the only way there was to go."

"I think she's right," Lindsay said, "I didn't see any other trails, either."

This was strange, Jane thought. If the map showed that the red trail led to the base of the cliff, and they followed the red trail, how had they ended up at a snake-infested dead end on top of the cliff?

"Maybe we misread the map," she said. "Let's look at it again."

"We can't," Lindsay said. "The ever-helpful Chelsea had it with her when she took off. We can check it when we get back to camp."

It was only four o'clock. They could have spent another hour exploring, but they headed back to Cabin 8. The encounter with the snakes had wiped Jane out.

When they reached the cabin, they found Chelsea lounging on her cot polishing her nails.

"What kept you guys?" she said. "Did you kids have fun playing in the woods?"

"What do you think you were doing, taking off like that?" Lindsay demanded angrily. "We're supposed to work together and help each other."

It was unsettling to have a team member you couldn't count on. Jane's dad always said a chain was only as strong as its weakest link.

Chelsea was nothing but dead weight, as far as the team was concerned. She contributed no ideas. She brought no useful equipment.

And when you really needed her, she was outta there.

Jane knew that Lindsay, when she was pushed, had a bad temper. But Jane preferred to avoid confrontation.

"Chelsea," she said, "why don't you just hand over the compass and map?"

"Take your stupid compass and map," Chelsea sneered. "It's in my leather fanny pack. My nails are wet, so you'll have to get it yourself. And don't touch anything else!"

She's the only snake around here worth worrying about, Jane thought. We'd be better off if she stayed out of our project altogether.

Molly was sitting closest to the fanny pack, so she reached over and unzipped it. She dug through some lipstick, a small atomizer of perfume, and a key ring before finding the compass and the map.

As Molly unfolded the map, she gasped.

Lindsay and Jane looked up.

"What is it Molly?" they asked in unison.

Molly was speechless. The color drained from her face. Her skin turned a ghostly white. Her eyes stayed riveted to the paper.

Lindsay and Jane ran over to see what had Molly so terrified. Jane looked over Molly's shoulder at the map.

Were her eyes deceiving her? She drew back in fear.

The top right hand corner of the map was pierced with two holes.

And down the page from each of them ran a thin red stream of blood.

Chapter Nine

Lindsay grabbed the map from Molly's hands and took it to the window.

"Relax you guys," she said. "Miss Priss over there probably just spilled her stupid nail polish on it."

She held the paper up to her nose and sniffed. Then she rolled her eyes and nodded.

"Nice going, Chelsea," she said. "Now our map is useless."

"Let me see it," Jane said. "We can still make out parts of it."

As she studied the map, Jane realized that the only parts still free of nail polish were the parts that were off limits.

Then she remembered the old mine, and thought of the mineral specimens they might find if they explored it.

She looked at the map. The nail polish did not obscure the trail they would have to take to reach the mine. Since today had been fruitless, they had some serious specimen hunting to do tomorrow.

The mine was their best hope.

She wondered if she could convince the others to bend the rules and visit a place that was off limits.

Lindsay, she knew, would be no problem. Lindsay always enjoyed taking a few risks. And the two of them could probably get Molly to agree.

Chelsea, however, was a different story. If she didn't agree to go, she could really mess them up. And Chelsea obviously didn't care at all about the success of their project.

But part of the assignment was to work as a team. If Chelsea refused to go with them, the whole team would suffer. Miss Farlie wouldn't care whose fault it was if they found no specimens. She would just know they hadn't completed the project.

Jane would have to think of a way to trick Chelsea into going to the mine.

But how?

Chapter Ten

With only an hour left before dinner, the girls decided to wash up. They grabbed towels and headed for the showers.

The shower room was behind the cabins; a footpath led the girls around back. When they rounded the corner of their cabin, they could not believe what they saw.

The shower room was nothing more than four half-walls around a slab of cement. Overhead, a long pipe with spray holes every couple of feet ran the length of the room. One faucet at the end turned on all the showers at once.

And the water from that one faucet was cold. Icy cold.

Nails stuck out of the shower walls, and the girls hung their towels on them.

Jane hadn't felt water this cold since she and Lindsay were little and ran under the sprinklers on hot summer days. Back then, it had felt good to run through such icy water.

Now it felt awful. Jane took the quickest shower in history.

As they were all drying off, she realized this would be a good chance to talk to Lindsay and Molly without Chelsea around. She had to clue them in on her plan.

"Listen you guys," she began, "if we don't find some good specimens tomorrow, our project will be a failure."

"What's your idea, Jane?" Lindsay asked.

"I say we explore that old mine," Jane said emphatically. She hoped the others would agree if she spoke firmly enough.

"But you said it was off limits," Molly said nervously. "Miss Farlie said don't go off limits. We could get in trouble."

"I don't mind going," Lindsay said. "But what about our Miss Chelsea? I bet she'll either refuse to go or tell on us."

"I've already thought about that," Jane said. "Let's not tell her where we're heading until it's too late. We've got the map now. We'll take charge and lead the way. She'll have no choice but to follow."

"What if she tells on us when we get back?" Molly asked.

"No problem," Jane said. "We'll show Miss Farlie how Chelsea wrecked our map with her nail polish. We'll say that, thanks to Chelsea, we couldn't read the map and took a wrong turn. If we get caught, we back up each other's story. Deal?"

"Deal," Lindsay said.

"Deal," Molly whispered.

Chapter Eleven

Jane, Lindsay and Molly walked back down the footpath from the showers to Cabin 8. They pushed open the door and found that Chelsea had already left.

Jane got ready for dinner and grabbed a sweatshirt for later on. Then she and the other two headed toward the flagpole to meet Alyssa, Katie, Jaimie and Carolyn.

"You all know Molly don't you?" Jane asked the others when they met.

She was starting to like Molly. Molly was quiet — but that was nice, sometimes. She was also helpful and reliable. Molly was a nerd, but Jane hoped her friends would be nice to her anyway.

All the girls looked at Molly and said, "Hi!"

Jane realized she had had nothing to worry

about. If she accepted Molly as a friend, that was good enough for the others.

Dinner was delicious. Maybe it was the country air. Or the fact they hadn't had a snack all afternoon. Maybe it was just being with their friends. Or maybe it was that Jane had never roasted a hot dog over an open fire before.

Jane thought she had never eaten such a delicious meal.

As they ate and talked, the sun set in the distance. The woods took on the beautiful glow of dusk. Stars appeared in the sky. Millions and billions of them.

Jane had never seen so many stars. She knew that the same stars sparkled in the sky whether you were at home or at camp. But in the suburbs, you never saw this many.

Cabins 4 and 12 had to do dinner clean-up. When the area was cleared of food and trash, everyone gathered in a huge circle around the campfire.

Miss Farlie made some announcements.

"The weather forecast for tomorrow is iffy,"

she began. "We may be in for some rain. If your group is going exploring, stay near the cabins. If you happen to be out hiking and we have a thunderstorm, take shelter and make your way back to camp as soon as you can. Before leaving in the morning, check in with me or the other teachers and let us know where you plan on heading."

Jane glanced nervously at Lindsay and Molly. This could spoil everything. If they had to tell Miss Farlie where they were heading, she wouldn't let them go.

They would just have to be vague.

Jane had to go to the bathroom. Going to the outhouse alone was OK in the daytime. At night, though, she wanted company.

"Hey Lindsay!" she whispered. "Will you come with me to the bathroom?"

"Sure, let's go," Lindsay said.

The outhouses stood alongside the showers, behind the cabins. Away from the glow of the campfire, the night was darker than the girls had realized. Lanterns hung from the backs of the cabins, but they didn't throw much light.

Jane felt her heart pounding in her chest. She did not like this at all. All her senses felt heightened as she strained to see through the inky blackness. Her nerves were on edge.

Keep calm, she thought. It's just like the daytime, only darker.

But she couldn't convince herself. She couldn't stop thinking that someone or something could be lurking in the darkness, ready to pounce on her.

She glanced at Lindsay. She looked nervous, too.

"Are you OK Lindsay?" Jane asked.

"Sure I am," Lindsay said. "I'm sure it was nothing anyway."

"*What* was nothing?" Jane asked.

"That noise. Didn't you hear it?"

"What did it sound like?" Jane asked. Her voice trembled and her throat felt tight.

"It was just some cracking sounds," Lindsay said. "Probably a squirrel."

They reached the outhouses. Small lanterns hung on each door. Lindsay and Jane each took one and went into side-by-side outhouses that shared a wall between them.

Suddenly, Jane heard a noise outside her door. She stayed still and didn't make a sound.

"What's that?" Lindsay whispered loudly through the wall.

"I don't know," Jane breathed. "But I'm not leaving until it stops!"

The noise sounded like a dog scratching on a door. It sounded like something sharp scraping against the outhouse door.

In their separate chambers, Lindsay and Jane stood frozen with fear, hardly daring to breathe. Jane was determined to stay in the outhouse as long as the scratching continued — even if it lasted all night.

After what seemed like an eternity, the sound stopped. Jane heard footsteps.

She no longer dared whisper to Lindsay, for fear of attracting attention.

Alone in the dark, she waited in fear.

Chapter Twelve

"Lindsay! Jane! Where are you? Are you guys OK?"

It was Molly's voice.

Jane pushed open the door to the outhouses. As she did, a gust of wind blew out her lantern.

She looked and saw that the wind had blown out Lindsay's light, too. The girls shrieked, grabbed each other, and ran back to the cabins, where the larger lanterns hung.

They stood there together under the light of the hanging lanterns. Lighting a stick with the flame of a big lantern, Lindsay re-lit their small lanterns.

They turned to Molly, who stood there out of breath from having run to keep up with them.

"Boy, were we glad to see you!" Jane exclaimed.

A smile spread across Molly's face. Jane wondered if Molly had ever heard those words before.

"You were away from the campfire so long, I thought I'd check on you," Molly said.

Lindsay and Jane hugged each other and shivered.

"Molly, did you see anyone run away from the outhouses?" Lindsay asked. "We heard footsteps."

"I didn't see a thing," Molly said. "You probably heard *my* footsteps."

Lindsay and Jane stayed huddled together for a moment, trying to catch their breath and calm down. But they needed to return the lanterns to the stall doors, so they started back toward the outhouses.

With every step, they glanced around nervously. They just wanted to make it to the hooks, hang up the lanterns and return to the safety of the group.

One more step and the hooks would be within their reach.

Jane raised her lantern to hang it on the hook — and stopped dead in her tracks.

She wanted to say something to Lindsay, but

she couldn't even speak. Slowly, she raised her hand and pointed to the door.

Lindsay turned to look and let out a blood-curdling scream.

Chapter Thirteen

Stay away from my m —

The message trailed off unfinished.

Could it have been there before? Jane stepped closer to the door and held the light up to take a better look.

People had carved many things into the out-house door over the years:

Brooke loves Jake.

Camp Armonk Rules.

DW & FB.

And lots more. But all those carvings looked like they had been there forever. Dirt had worked its way into the letters and darkened them.

The message Jane saw now looked freshly carved. Light-colored curls of wood hung from each letter.

Lindsay held her lantern near the ground. Splinters of wood lay on the pine needles.

Someone had just done this.

Someone had been watching Lindsay and Jane, had followed them to the outhouses, and had scratched out this message in the door. Someone who wanted them to stay away from something.

But what?

"Maybe Chelsea and her friends are up to their old tricks," Lindsay said.

"But what could it mean?" Jane asked. "What could they want us to stay away from?"

"Well," Molly said, "Chelsea told us not to touch any of her stuff."

"That's true," Jane said. "Maybe it was just Chelsea trying to scare us."

Jane was happy to blame this on Chelsea. The alternatives were too frightening to consider. She convinced herself, and breathed a sigh of relief.

The three girls headed back to the campfire. The group was singing a round.

Jane couldn't concentrate on the words. She

scanned the crowd, looking over the sea of singing faces until she spotted Chelsea sitting on a log.

She looks so relaxed, Jane thought. She doesn't look the slightest bit guilty, or even pleased with herself — at least no more pleased with herself than usual. If she had done it, wouldn't she look at us to see our reaction? Wouldn't she gloat?

It had comforted Jane to think that Chelsea was responsible for the warning carved on the outhouse door. Now it looked as if she'd had nothing to do with it.

Her mind whirled. Then who *had* carved the warning? And what did it mean?

Miss Farlie broke up the campfire meeting at 9:30 and sent everyone back to their cabins. As Jane got ready for bed, she eyed Chelsea suspiciously, looking for some sign of guilt. She thought she saw a trace of a smirk on Chelsea's face, though she wasn't sure.

But then she remembered how Chelsea had acted after she'd scared the dickens out of Jane by using a coat hanger as a snake.

Chelsea had been so pleased with herself she couldn't wait to tell her friends.

Jane realized that Chelsea couldn't have carved the message. If she had, she and her friends would have been enjoying a good laugh over it by now. Heck, Chelsea would probably be re-enacting her stunt.

That could mean only one thing. Someone *else* was trying to stop her and her friends from doing something.

But what? What should they stay away from?

Jane unrolled her sleeping bag, spread it on the cot and climbed in. It felt so soft and warm inside. She felt safe and secure and snug.

Then it hit her like a ton of bricks. A chill ran through her, and her skin began to crawl.

She knew now what the carver had been trying to say.

Stay away from my MINE!

Chapter Fourteen

"Lindsay!" Jane whispered. She didn't want to wake the others.

She got no response. Lindsay had already fallen asleep.

I'll just have to wait for morning to tell her what I think the sign means, Jane thought.

She tried not to think about the carved message. She tried not to think about the snakes. She tried not to think about the cliff and the miss-marked trail.

But the harder she tried not to think of scary things, the more scary her thoughts became. She tossed and turned for what seemed like forever.

Finally sleep came.

*　　*　　*

61

Light filtered in through the small, dirty window of the cabin.

Jane opened her eyes. She felt like she had only slept for five minutes.

Glancing around the room, she saw that Molly was awake, reading in bed. Chelsea was still sleeping, and proving it by snoring loudly. Jane looked over at Lindsay's bed.

It was empty.

"Psst, Molly," Jane whispered. "Where's Lindsay?"

"I don't know," Molly whispered back. "Her bed was empty when I woke up."

Chelsea stopped snoring, writhed around on her cot, moaned, then opened her eyes and glared at them.

"Do you think you could talk any louder?" she barked.

Jane did not reply. What was the point? The girl was too rude for words.

Suddenly, the cabin door burst open and Lindsay flew in breathlessly.

"You guys are never going to believe this!" she shouted.

"What is this, Grand Central Station?" Chelsea snapped. "I'm outta here!" She leapt out of bed, grabbed her towel and clothes, and stormed out of the cabin.

"Good," said Lindsay. "Now that she's gone I can tell you what I saw. You won't believe it."

"You said that already," Jane said. "Now tell us!"

"Well," Lindsay began, still trying to catch her breath. "I had to go to the outhouse this morning, and I wanted to check the message. You know, to make sure it really happened. I went back to the same one you were in last night Jane, and get this: *There was no message*! *Nothing*! I mean, the old messages were still there, but not the fresh one we all saw last night."

She paused and looked at them.

"We *did* all see it, right?" she asked, her voice anxious.

"Of course we all saw it," Jane said. "After you all fell asleep last night, I thought of what the message could mean. I think the last word was *mine*. Stay away from my *MINE*."

"But no one but the three of us knew we planned to go to the mine," Molly said.

They all looked at each other. No one said a word.

Jane thought about the strange message, and she thought about the miss-marked trail, too. Clearly, *someone* knew they wanted to explore the mine, and was trying desperately to stop them.

She was usually a bit on the timid side, at least compared to Lindsay. But now she felt determined.

"Look," she said. "We've put a lot of work into this project, right? We can't afford to let someone scare us out of a good grade for no reason."

The other girls looked at her and nodded. They talked it over a bit longer, and everyone agreed — whoever or whatever was responsible for these mysterious happenings was not going to stand in their way.

Together, the three of them would take on their opposition, whatever it turned out to be.

Just then, they heard a knock on the cabin door. The door swung open, and in walked Miss Farlie.

"Good morning, ladies," she said, sounding as if she'd been awake for hours. "What's your plan for today?"

Jane and Lindsay exchanged a quick glance. Jane swallowed, and spoke up.

"Uh, we're going to explore the base of the cliff along the red trail," she said. "We figure there will be lots of rock specimens there."

"Sounds good, ladies," Miss Farlie said. She made a note on her clipboard and started to leave.

"Miss Farlie," Jane said. "Would it be OK if we took our lunch with us? I know we're supposed to check in for meals, but we hardly accomplished anything yesterday, We have a lot planned for today."

Miss Farlie thought a moment, then said, "I guess that will be all right. Just remember what I said about the weather. The skies are overcast, so be alert. If it starts to rain, head right back to camp. Have fun."

With that, she left.

"Well that was easy," Lindsay said. "You sounded totally cool, Jane."

"I was kind of nervous," Jane replied. "I'm glad it didn't show in my voice."

Suddenly, Chelsea stormed back into the cabin.

"Let's get something straight, lame-brains," she snapped. "Tomorrow morning, whoever wakes me up will pay for it dearly. Got it?"

"We're trembling with fear Chelsea," Lindsay said, and rolled her eyes. "Just get ready to go. We're leaving in a few minutes — with or without you."

Everyone bustled around the cabin. They gathered the things they thought they'd need — flashlights, canteens, bug spray, notebooks, pencils, and plastic bags for collecting rocks and minerals — and crammed them into their packs.

Jane suggested they take ponchos. Lindsay grabbed her pocketknife and slipped it into a pocket on the side of her backpack.

"We're not supposed to have weapons at school," Chelsea said.

"First of all," Lindsay said, "this is not a

weapon. Second of all, we're not *in* school. Third of all, mind your own business or I may be tempted to see if it makes a good weapon."

"Now *I'm* trembling with fear," Chelsea said. She pretended to shake all over.

Lindsay ignored Chelsea, finished packing her gear and asked if everyone was ready to get breakfast.

The four headed to the flagpole area, ate a quick meal, grabbed their sack lunches and headed for the red trail.

Chapter Fifteen

It took a while for Chelsea to realize they were heading down the same trail they had taken the day before.

Suddenly, she seemed to get her mind off herself for a moment and look around at her surroundings.

"Hey morons!" she snapped. "This is the way we went yesterday. Do you want to get lost again?"

"We won't get lost," Jane replied. "Here's the turn-off now."

They were less than fifty yards from the top of the trail. Jane pointed to an overgrown path splitting off to the side. When she examined a tree at the turn-off, she spotted a small piece of a red blaze stuck under a nail.

"It looks like someone tried to rip down this

trail marker," she said. "There's only a fragment left."

"No wonder we missed it yesterday," Lindsay said. "This must be the right way to go."

The girls fell into single file, with Lindsay leading the way.

The trail hadn't been groomed in a long time. The girls were thankful they were wearing long pants. Twigs and brush stuck out into the narrow path and scratched against their jeans.

They hiked in silence.

It took a lot of concentration to hike this trail. They had to scramble over fallen logs, skirt mud holes, and keep their balance on the loose rocks underfoot. After about twenty minutes, they emerged into a clearing and found themselves staring up at the rocky cliff.

They were standing right below the spot they had ended up in yesterday. That meant they should, right now, be standing in front of the tree they had seen from above — the one marked with the red blaze.

Jane glanced at the tree and gasped.

All that remained of the red blaze was a tiny

piece stuck under a nail.

Someone had ripped this marker down, too. Someone who did not want them on this trail.

Someone who knew of their plan and was one step ahead of them.

Molly seemed oblivious to these worries. Jane saw her spot some sparkling stones on the ground and collect a few samples.

Chelsea lounged against the rocks looking bored.

"Well, I see our little Molly has gotten some pretty rocks, so let's head back now," she said, and yawned.

"We've only just begun," Jane replied.

Chelsea made a face, but she came with them. They headed further down the trail, past the cliff, and toward their real destination.

The mine.

Chapter Sixteen

Chelsea sighed loudly as she walked. She was clearly uncomfortable, and she wanted everyone to know. She ducked branches and swatted flies. And sighed some more.

She did not seem to realize they were heading to the off-limits area.

"Do any of you Camp Fire Girls know where in the heck we're going?" she moaned. "This overgrown path is probably not even on the map."

Jane guessed from the way the trail had been climbing that they must be close to the entrance to the mine.

"Quit complaining, Chelsea," Lindsay said. "We know where we are. What do you say we all take a rest and eat some of our lunch?"

Everyone, even Chelsea, agreed with this suggestion. They took out their canteens and inspected their sack lunches hungrily.

Whoever had packed them sure knew what kids liked!

Each girl had a sandwich on a roll piled high with turkey, cheese and lettuce. They had little packets of mustard and mayonnaise. They each had a bag of chips, a very chocolaty brownie, and a bag of trail mix.

Jane decided to eat half of her lunch now and save the rest for later. Chelsea refused to eat anything but the turkey and lettuce.

"She'll eat when she gets hungry enough," Lindsay said. "My brothers are picky eaters. But when we go camping, they get so hungry my mom can get them to try anything!"

As they started to pack up what remained of their food, Jane noticed her canteen was missing. She had just taken a drink and put it down by her backpack.

Now it was gone.

"Hey you guys, did anyone pick up my canteen by mistake?" she asked.

"No," Lindsay said. "Mine's right . . . " Her voice trailed off.

Hers was missing too.

"Mine's gone too!" Molly said.

The girls scoured the area. How could three canteens just disappear? They looked accusingly at Chelsea.

"Why are you all looking at me?" Chelsea snapped. "I wouldn't touch one of your dirty canteens if I was dying of thirst in the Sahara."

Under protest, Chelsea let them look in her pack. The canteens were not there.

This was weird. How could you lose something as big as a canteen? Even weirder, how could you lose *three* of them?

Jane thought someone was trying to sabotage their project. If it was Chelsea, she was not working alone.

And if it was not Chelsea, they could be in real danger.

Chapter Seventeen

The girls pressed on.

They were spooked by the disappearance of their water supply, but not spooked enough to turn around.

The trail narrowed. They could barely find footing.

Chelsea griped loudly, but the others were determined and they ignored her complaints.

Soon, they emerged into a small clearing. There in front of them, they saw it — an old boarded up mine.

Suddenly, the sky cracked with lightning. Thunder rumbled in their ears.

The girls looked up and saw that the sky had become almost as black as night. The trail they had taken was so overgrown they hadn't noticed the clouds roll in.

Another bolt of lightning flashed across the sky, almost blinding them. Thunder boomed, closer this time.

"We'd better go back to camp," Molly said, her voice trembling.

"We can't go back in a storm like this," Lindsay said. "We'd better take cover and wait it out."

"We have to find a way into the mine, and take cover in there," Jane said. She was so excited to be at the mine, she could barely stand it.

The mine was boarded shut, but the boards looked old and weathered. Lindsay found a loose piece of wood and used it to pry off a couple of the boards. Soon she had made an opening large enough to crawl through.

The rain was just starting as they scrambled, one by one, into the darkness. As soon as they were inside, the air was lit by the brightest flash of lightning yet. Thunder rattled the loose boards.

As the flash illuminated the mine, Jane glanced around to get her bearings. But the light vanished too quickly, leaving the girls in pitch darkness.

"I remember learning in science that when thunder and lightning happen really close together, it means you're near the center of the storm," Molly said, her voice quavering. "I hope it blows by quickly."

"We might as well make the most of it while we're in here," Jane said, trying to sound cheerful.

She was scared and cold, but she was excited, too. After all, she had wanted to come here. They were finally going to explore the mine, and they'd probably find some great specimens.

It would be worth all the anxiety if she could bring home a chunk of gold!

Lindsay, Molly and Jane took out their flashlights, put on their sweatshirts, and began looking around, as their eyes adjusted to darkness.

Chelsea did not have a flashlight. She grabbed the hood of Lindsay sweatshirt to stop her from walking away. Then she tried to grab her flashlight.

"Hands off, Chelsea!" Lindsay said, sounding as if now she had been pushed too far. "If you weren't smart enough to bring your own flashlight, that's *your* problem. You can follow me, but *I'm* holding the light."

Chelsea must have been really scared, because she didn't even snap back at Lindsay.

Jane could make out three passageways into the mine. The one to the right had metal tracks on the ground, the kind of tracks along which a small cart could be pushed.

Jane convinced the others to choose that one. The four of them headed into the tunnel, the waving beams of their flashlights their only weapon against the inky darkness.

Chapter Eighteen

The air in the tunnel was damp and cold.

The girls walked carefully, in silence, with Lindsay leading the way. Chelsea clung to Lindsay's hood. Jane and Molly brought up the rear.

"I'll bet this was a gold mine," Molly whispered.

Jane had been thinking the same thing. In doing her research for the trip, she had read about discoveries of gold in the area.

That had been a hundred years ago, though. Would anything remain after all that time?

Common sense told her not to expect to find gold. After all, men had killed each other over gold. She felt pretty sure that, if this had been a gold mine, nobody would have left any gold in it.

The flashlights lit their way enough for them to

see where they were stepping, but little more. Every few minutes, Lindsay stopped and shined her light down the tunnel to see what was ahead. Jane and Molly shined their lights overhead and to the sides, searching for shiny spots in the walls.

All they saw was a long, dark, wet, cold tunnel. Not a speck of gold.

Slowly, they followed Lindsay into the blackness. They heard dripping in the distance, a steady drip, drip, drip that sounded like the bathroom sink at Jane's house. If you didn't tighten the faucet in her bathroom, the dripping could keep you up all night.

She wondered whether a creek ran through the cave. Gold was often found near water. She'd seen people in old movies panning for gold by the sides of rivers.

She started to get excited again.

Then she heard a scream.

The flashlight ahead went out. Jane and Molly pointed their flashlights ahead and gasped.

Lindsay and Chelsea had vanished.

Jane stopped in her tracks and began calling

for them.

There was no reply.

"Shine your light right at the ground, Molly," Jane said, her voice shaking in the darkness. "I'm going to look ahead."

Cautiously, she crept forward. Molly stayed frozen in place.

Jane took the tiniest baby steps imaginable. Then she stopped to listen. Tiny step. Stop. Tiny step. Stop. Freeze.

A low moan hung in the air ahead. Then she heard another moan.

Slowly, she moved the beam of her flashlight in a circle, looking for the source of the moan.

She saw nothing.

She turned her head to check on Molly. Molly was still there, still rooted in the same spot. Still petrified.

Suddenly, something grabbed Jane's leg. She screamed.

Chapter Nineteen

Jane's scream jolted Molly into action.

She raced to Jane's side and shined her light at Jane's face. Jane's mouth hung open. Her eyes were wide with fear.

"S-s-s-something is on my l-l-leg," she sputtered.

Molly pointed her light toward the ground. The moaning grew louder. Fearfully, Jane looked down.

Lindsay was on the ground, clinging to Jane's leg. She looked hurt.

Jane knelt by her friend, then let out a gasp.

For the first time she saw what lay ahead. One more step and she would have fallen into a hole. The same hole out of which Lindsay had been trying to crawl when she latched onto Jane's leg.

Jane grabbed the back of Lindsay's jeans and pulled her out of the hole. They hugged. Tears rolled down Jane's face.

"I thought you were hurt or dead!" she cried. "I thought I'd lost my best friend. Are you all right?"

"I'm OK," Lindsay answered. "Just a little shaken up."

The moaning began again. Louder than ever. And more obnoxious.

"We'd better get Chelsea out of there or we'll never hear the end of it," Lindsay said.

Molly and Jane shined their lights into the hole. It wasn't too deep, but it seemed to stretch on forever.

Jane realized this wasn't a hole at all. The metal tracks ended abruptly where they stood, yet the passageway continued after the drop-off.

With a sigh, Lindsay lowered herself back down. The others followed. All three of them helped Chelsea to her feet.

She was filthy and sore, but not seriously harmed.

"When we get out of here, *if* we get out of

here, you three are dead!" she snarled.

Ignoring Chelsea, Lindsay began looking for her flashlight. She had dropped it when she had fallen.

"Hey Jane, shine your light around so I can find my flashlight," she said. "It's got to be around here somewhere."

Molly and Jane shined their lights on the ground.

At the start of the lower section, the passage-way was about three feet wide. A few feet ahead, it narrowed to two feet.

They didn't see any holes or crevices for a flashlight to roll into. But they couldn't find it any-where.

"It's too cold to just stand around," Chelsea muttered. "Forget the stupid flashlight and let's get out of here."

Jane hated to admit it, but Chelsea was right. If they didn't keep moving, they would freeze. But if they gave up the search, they would have only two flashlights left for the four of them. Not great.

Then she got an idea.

First, she got Molly to shine her flashlight on the ground. Then she put her own flashlight down in the beam of light.

As she expected, her flashlight began to roll along the ground, farther into the tunnel.

The passageway sloped downward! They had climbed up to get to the entrance to the mine. Now the tunnel was taking them back down into the depths of the mountain.

The girls had to walk quickly to keep up with the rolling flashlight. They followed until it came to a stop — right alongside Lindsay's.

Jane was psyched. Her plan had worked.

She might not be as experienced at this stuff as Lindsay. Still, she decided, she was turning out to be quite a camper after all.

<u>Chapter Twenty</u>

Lindsay bent down to grab the flashlights. She handed one to Jane, then reached for her own.

"Jane, shine your light back this way for a minute," she said. "I just brushed up against something strange."

A hush fell over the group. On the ground next to Lindsay's flashlight lay a brown leather box. Wrapped around it were two leather straps with brass buckles.

Jane knelt to get a closer look. The box was partly covered by an oily canvas cloth. She lifted the cloth and peered beneath it.

It looked as if someone had tried to dig a hole and hide the box inside.

Jane and Lindsay removed the cloth and lifted the box out of the shallow pit. Molly shined her light on the box. A padlock gleamed in the darkness.

The leather straps were merely decorative. An iron padlock, with a very large keyhole, held the lid in place.

There was no key in sight.

"I wonder what's inside?" Jane said. "We've got to find a way to open it."

"Maybe we can smash the lock with a rock," Molly suggested.

Chelsea leaned forward to look. "Or we could use Lindsay's weapon — I mean pocketknife," she said.

Jane looked at Chelsea in surprise. Could it be? Was Chelsea actually contributing something besides snide remarks?

"I can't believe I'm saying this," Lindsay said. "But good thinking Chelsea."

Lindsay rifled through her backpack and found the knife.

"Here Chelsea, you hold this," she said, handing over her flashlight. A small smile crept over Chelsea's face. She seemed pleased to become part of the adventure.

Lindsay tried various tools from the pocket-knife. Nothing worked. She gave an exasperated sigh. Jane thought Lindsay looked about ready to give up.

Suddenly, a loud crash shook the ground and knocked Lindsay off her feet.

Clouds of dust flew around, forcing the girls to cover their faces as they crouched on the ground. It took a few seconds for the noise to die down.

When the dust settled, the girls shined their lights all around to see what had happened. What they saw left them speechless.

Not five feet from where they crouched, back in the direction from which they had come, a huge pile of rocks and debris blocked the tunnel. Small stones began tumbling down the path toward them, followed by larger ones.

"We've got to get out of here or we'll be buried alive!" Chelsea screamed.

They scrambled to their feet and ran farther into the darkness. Lindsay, the only one not holding a flashlight, snatched the leather box and sprinted down the passageway.

The beams from their flashlights jumped around the tunnel. The girls didn't stop moving until the path took a sharp turn.

Jane stopped to catch her breath. Behind her, Lindsay rounded the corner, tripped on a rock and fell on her face. The box flew out of her arms, smashed into the wall, fell to the ground, and spilled its contents at their feet.

All four of them stared in disbelief.

Chapter Twenty-One

"Now this is more like it!" Chelsea exclaimed. She hadn't sounded so happy since she had fooled Jane about the snakes.

Gold and jewels covered the ground. The girls gazed at diamond rings, emerald earrings, sapphire pendants, strands of pearls, and hundreds of loose gems of every size and shape imaginable.

Jane had never seen anything like it.

For a few moments they all stood frozen, too awestruck to move. Then Chelsea dropped to her knees and began running her fingers through all of the jewels.

"Are you all right Lindsay?" Jane asked.

Lindsay had not stood up since her fall.

"I'm OK, I guess," Lindsay said. "I can't believe what I'm seeing, though."

"Believe it," Molly said quietly, "Unless we're all having the same dream, there are millions of dollars worth of jewels here."

Jane didn't know a lot about jewelry. She had a gold locket her grandparents had given her when she was born, a pair of opal earrings they'd given her on her seventh birthday, and a gold bracelet from some family friends.

They weren't much, but from the way her mother carried on about not losing them, you would have thought it was worth a fortune.

Sometimes she and Lindsay would look at jewelry in the windows at the mall. The big fancy stuff — the stuff like the gems spread over the floor of the mine — was expensive.

Very expensive. That much she did know.

"Where do you suppose it came from?" Jane asked.

"I don't know," Lindsay said. "But now I see why someone wanted us to stay away from here."

"What do you mean?" Chelsea asked. "Who wanted us to stay away from here?"

Jane and Lindsay looked at each other, and shrugged. Then they looked at Molly.

"We'd better tell her," Molly said.

"Tell me what, dork?" Chelsea snapped, sounding a lot more like her old self again.

Jane told Chelsea about the mysterious warning carved on the outhouse door. She told her, too, about her realization that the trail had been marked wrong the day of their first hike. And she told her about the sabotaging of the trail again today, when someone had removed the red blazes.

Then she reminded Chelsea about how their canteens had disappeared.

Chelsea's face turned red.

"Are you telling me that, with all this creepy stuff happening, you tricked me into coming here?" she fumed.

"Look, Chelsea, we thought *you* might be the one responsible," Lindsay said. "You got such a kick out of scaring Jane when she was under the cabin, we thought you might be doing this other stuff, too."

"Listen you guys," Jane interrupted. "We have

better things to do than argue about why we're here. Let's pick this stuff up and find a way out. We can fight later."

The four of them got down on their hands and knees to sweep the spilled treasure back into the box. Out of the corner of her eye, Jane saw Chelsea sneak a sapphire and diamond ring into the pocket of her blue jeans.

When everything was back in the box, Jane swept her flashlight around to be sure they hadn't missed anything. No jewels sparkled on the ground. The floor of the passageway was just as they had found it — cold, bare dirt.

Then her light flashed over a yellowish square of paper lying on the ground. She bent to pick it up.

It appeared to be a very old piece of newspaper, neatly folded into quarters.

Carefully, so as not to tear it, she unfolded the paper, looked at the news article — and gasped in horror at the words she read:

Couple Slain in Multimillion Dollar Robbery.

Chapter Twenty-Two

The first paragraph of the news story said that no leads had been found in the double murder of the millionaire Louis Armonk and his wife, Emily. The couple had been murdered in their sleep and the thief had taken off with Emily's massive jewel collection, leaving no clues.

"You guys, this is stolen stuff!" Jane exclaimed. "The newspaper is dated from fifty years ago. These jewels have been hidden in here for fifty years!"

"Did you notice the names of the victims," Molly asked.

Jane looked again. Armonk.

The victims of this terrible crime had the same name as the camp. This was their mine and their camp.

And these were their jewels.

The girls were spooked. They had wanted to

get out of the mine even before Jane had found the newspaper. Now they were desperate.

Jane felt her heart pounding in her throat. She slipped the newspaper into her back pocket, and looked around for a way out.

Since the rock slide blocked them from getting out the way they had come, they headed further into the mine, deeper into the blackness. They had no other choice, no other way to go.

Lindsay and Molly led the way. Chelsea carried the box.

Jane followed. Maybe, she thought, the tunnel would connect with one of the others they had seen at the entrance. Then, if they turned the right way, they could follow that tunnel until they found their way out.

Sticking close together, the girls walked slowly forward. Lindsay proceeded cautiously, looking as if she feared falling into another hole.

Molly shone her light high, while Lindsay aimed hers low. The tunnel grew even narrower than before.

The path leveled off. The girls had to stoop to

get through.

Lindsay stopped walking, and Molly smacked right into her.

"What's the matter Lindsay?" Molly asked. "Why did you stop?"

"I can barely stand up straight anymore," Lindsay said. "If the tunnel gets any shorter, we'll have to crawl."

"Nice going, lame-brains," Chelsea said. "Now what do we do?"

"I don't think we have any choice," Jane said. "We know we can't go back, so we have to try going forward. Maybe the opening will get taller again."

The girls kept on going. Soon, they had to drop to their hands and knees and crawl. Chelsea pushed the leather box on the ground ahead of her. Jane smiled grimly as she heard the box scrape along the ground. Chelsea might be afraid and whiny, but no way did she intend to leave that box behind.

They crawled for what seemed like forever.

Then Lindsay shouted, "It's ending! The tunnel is ending!" There was panic in her voice.

Jane felt herself tense up. Lindsay was usually the calm one. If *she* was panicking, they were in trouble.

Jane looked forward to see what Lindsay was panicked about.

Right in front of them, the passageway opened into a little space into which two of them could fit.

But it was a dead end.

Chapter Twenty-Three

Molly crawled up next to Lindsay. Peering in through the opening, Jane saw the two of them squatting side by side in the little space at the end of the tunnel.

With both of them in there, it was crowded. The walls seemed to press in on them. They couldn't turn around, unless they did it together.

Molly backed out of the space.

The girls stopped and talked about what to do. If they had to retrace their steps, they would have to crawl backwards until they reached the part of the tunnel where they could stand up and turn around.

But why go back? The rock slide had blocked them in!

They could try to move the rocks and open up

the passageway. But who knew what else might come tumbling down on them?

They were cold, scared, tired, hungry and thirsty.

Then Lindsay spoke again, from inside the small space. She sounded excited.

"There's a hole in here!" she shouted, her voice echoing off the rock walls of the tunnel. "We can get out! Come on in, one at a time."

Molly crawled back into the small space. Then she was gone.

Then Chelsea disappeared into the space, carrying the leather box. Jane was alone in the tunnel. Quickly, she wriggled into the little space.

She noticed a gleam of light from above and twisted her neck to get a better look.

There she saw Lindsay, about four feet up, sticking her head out of a hole in the wall of the tunnel.

Slowly, she got off her hands and knees and tried to stand up. She hadn't realized how stiff she had become in the tunnel. It felt good to stand and stretch her legs.

Lindsay reached out to help her. Jane grabbed Lindsay's arm. She tried to find footholds in the wall as Lindsay pulled her from above.

Before she could reach the safety of the upper tunnel, Jane felt something grip her ankle.

She screamed.

Startled, Lindsay let go of Jane's hand. Jane slipped back down, but Lindsay lurched forward and grabbed her by the sleeve.

"Grab my feet Molly," Lindsay shouted, leaning far out of the hole to hang on to Jane. She had a better grip now and she began tugging furiously on Jane's arms.

Jane kept screaming. She felt something pulling her back into the lower tunnel. She struggled to free herself.

"Help me, Lindsay," she screamed. "Help me!"

Lindsay struggled and grunted. Then, with one final tug, she freed Jane from the grasp of her attacker and dragged her into the upper tunnel.

The girls began furiously kicking rocks and dirt

back into the hole to stop whoever it was from following them.

After a few seconds, Jane caught her breath. The girls looked around, and made a dash down the tunnel.

About twenty feet further along, they came to a fork.

They didn't want to make a mistake, but they had no time to think.

Chelsea was in the lead, carrying the treasure box. She chose the left fork.

The others followed, and hoped that luck was on their side.

Chapter Twenty-Four

Jane ran until her legs felt like jelly.

Finally, all of them, gasping for air, stopped. They stood perfectly still, listening intently for any sounds other than their own heavy breathing.

They heard nothing.

Jane felt more frightened than ever before in her life. Her heart pounded wildly in her chest, and her throat felt so tight she could hardly breathe. This was way worse than snakes.

She began to wonder if they would make it out alive.

It was way past lunch time. But, because they had warned her, Miss Farlie did not expect them to check in at the flagpole. No one would know they were missing. No one would know that they were in trouble.

No one would come to help them.

Jane remembered her mother's last words to her: "Now remember honey, don't go wandering off with Lindsay and get lost. I don't want to get a call that something happened to you or hear that you caused the teachers any trouble."

As she stood in the darkness of the mine, Jane felt ashamed. Usually she was a good kid, one who followed the rules.

If she could just get out of this alive, she thought, she would never disobey her mother again.

She would never lie to her teacher again.

She would never trick another kid again.

If she could just get out of this alive, she would go back to her old ways.

The girls, hearing nothing following them, decided to move on and try to find a way out of the mine as quickly as they could.

Walking in a tight group, they shined their lights on the ground ahead of them and noticed metal tracks — the same kind they had followed into the mine.

Perhaps these tracks would lead them to safety.

The tunnel climbed slowly, leading them uphill. Jane hoped this was a good sign. When they had entered the mine, the tunnel had gone downhill, the way the flashlights had rolled, into the center of the mine. Since this path was heading up, maybe it would lead them out.

Jane didn't care if thunder and lightning were still crashing outside. She preferred to face a hurricane than whoever, or whatever, had grabbed her leg.

Chelsea still led the way. Jane and Molly came next. Lindsay walked behind them.

Jane noted that Lindsay turned every few seconds to shine her flashlight behind them. Lindsay was usually the adventurous one, but she seemed as nervous as a cat.

Once, as Jane looked back at her friend, she saw Lindsay pull her knife out of her pocket and keep it ready in her hand. Maybe it would serve as a weapon after all.

Suddenly, Jane crashed into Molly, who had crashed into Chelsea, who had stopped. Then Lindsay, who had been looking backwards, crashed into Jane.

"What's up, you guys?" Lindsay asked.

"There's a cart up here," Chelsea answered in a loud whisper. "It's blocking the whole tunnel."

"It looks like a tram," Molly said. "They probably used it to carry the gold out of the mine."

"Can't you squeeze around it?" Lindsay asked.

"No way," Chelsea said. "It's too tight."

Lindsay squeezed past Jane and Molly to get a better look. She gave the tram a big shove. It wouldn't budge. The others leaned into it with her, and they all pushed together.

Nothing happened. Their way was still blocked.

"Let's just climb in it and then climb out the other side," Lindsay said.

She hoisted herself up into the tram. Jane pushed past Chelsea and jumped in next. She wasn't going to be the last one in this time. Molly scrambled in after Jane.

Chelsea tried to climb in but couldn't make it with the leather box in her hand. Reluctantly, she handed the box to Lindsay, then lifted herself onto the edge of the tram and swung one leg over.

Just then, they felt a jolt. The tram loosened and began to roll.

"Help!" Chelsea shouted.

She was only halfway into the tram. The sudden motion made her lose her balance.

"I'm going to fall out," she yelled. "I'm going to lose the treasure!"

Chapter Twenty-Five

Chelsea's lust for the treasure seemed to give her superhuman strength. She clung to the tram with her fingernails and somehow regained her hold.

Lindsay helped pull Chelsea's other leg into the tram. Chelsea tumbled into the tram, grabbed the leather box, and hugged it like a long lost puppy.

The tram gained speed. It rolled down the tracks faster and faster. Jane remembered with horror that the first set of tracks had ended abruptly when the tunnel dropped off.

If these tracks ended the same way, with the tram going this fast, who knew what would happen to them?

She envisioned a pile of broken girls, beautifully adorned with the world's largest jewel collection.

It was not a pretty sight.

They pointed their flashlights ahead of the tram, but it was hard to see anything. The tunnel twisted and turned, and rose and fell. They picked up speed every time the tunnel dipped, then slowed when they came to a hill.

Eventually, the tunnel leveled off and the tram slowed down.

"Look," Lindsay said. He pointed at some ropes hanging along the side of the passageway.

"Everyone, when I count to three, reach out and grab onto a rope," she said. "Jane and Molly, you each grab one on the left. Chelsea and I will grab one on the right. When you get ahold of one, wrap it around your hand and hold on tight. We can stop this thing!"

Jane got ready to drop her light, as did Molly and Lindsay. Chelsea carefully placed the box on the floor of the tram, and straddled it with her feet.

"One . . . two . . . three . . . *grab!*" Lindsay shouted.

Everyone dropped their flashlights. The tunnel

darkened. They reached out through the blackness, trying to grab the ropes. Jane, groping in the dark like a blind person, felt one touch her hand. It was thick and rough, but she held on.

She wrapped the rope around her hand, planted her feet firmly on the floor of the tram, and leaned back with all her might. She could not see around her, but the grunts of her friends told her they were doing the same.

The tram kept rolling. Jane felt as if her arms were being stretched on a rack, but she held on tight. She closed her eyes and strained against the rope. It coiled so tightly around her hand she feared the circulation was cut off.

Finally, the tram ground to a halt.

Jane breathed a sigh of relief and groped for her flashlight.

Then she noticed a faint light just ahead.

"Look," she said. "Do you think maybe that's a way . . . "

None of them dared say it, for fear of getting their hopes up. One by one they climbed out of the tram. Chelsea passed the treasure box to Lindsay and then climbed out herself. They walked quickly toward the light.

As they got closer, the light got brighter.

"It *must* be a way out!" Jane shouted. "Hurry up, you guys!"

In less than a minute, the girls reached an opening to the mine. It wasn't the same way they had come in, but it was definitely a way out, and that was good enough.

Standing in the opening, Jane looked around trying to take it all in.

The tram tracks ended right where they stood. If Lindsay hadn't thought of grabbing onto the ropes, the tram would have kept going and dumped them right out of the tunnel.

Jane looked down and noticed what lay just beyond the opening.

Nothing.

The four girls stood on the edge of a cliff. The tram would have sailed out of the tunnel and crashed far below.

Leaning out of the opening and over the cliff, Jane noticed something else.

"Hey you guys, check this out," she said, pointing down below. "There's the tree with the torn-off red marker. We must be just above the mine entrance."

"That means we must be up on the rocky cliff we were on yesterday!" Lindsay said.

"That means," Jane said, her voice starting to shake, "there must be *snakes* around here."

Just then, from deep inside the tunnel, a ghostly, echoing voice called out: "Leave all the treasure and leave in peace," the voice said. "Take it and *die*!"

A shiver ran up Jane's spine. The voice sounded like one of those recordings in the haunted house she went to at Halloween.

There, it was fun. Here, it was terrifying.

"Let's get out of here!" Molly quavered. She reached around the opening to the tunnel and started inching her way to safety.

Jane followed right behind her.

"Come on, Chelsea," Lindsay urged. "Just leave the box, and let's go."

"Are you nuts?" Chelsea snapped. "I'm not leaving this treasure." She clutched the box to her chest.

"Look, Chelsea," Lindsay said. "If you hold onto the box, you can't make it out of the opening without falling off the cliff. Besides, can't you take a hint? Something creepy is warning us not to take it. So put it down and let's *go*!"

The eerie voiced echoed from the tunnel again. "Leave all the treasure and leave in peace. Take it and *die*!"

Reluctantly, Chelsea put the box on the ground. Then she followed Lindsay around the rocky opening to the exact spot where, the day before, Jane had encountered all the snakes.

The girls looked down, and still there — writhing in a sickening mass — they saw the snakes.

Chapter Twenty-Six

Carefully, the girls stepped around the snakes.

Rain spattered their faces and gathered in puddles on the top of the cliff. Between the snakes and the puddles, the girls found few good places to step.

Jane chose puddles over snakes. Her feet got wetter with each step. The rocks felt slick and very slippery.

She moved slowly and carefully. In a few minutes, she managed to ease her way by the sharp crag, scramble over the boulder, and get back to the start of the trail.

The trail to Cabin 8. The trail to safety.

Just then, lightning lit the sky and thunder crashed overhead.

Jane knew the woods were a bad place to be in a thunderstorm. But she thought a haunted mine was worse.

The girls looked at each other and started to run down the trail. The ground was wet and slippery. Molly fell and got covered with mud.

If they hadn't been so spooked, they would have laughed at how she looked. But not now.

Rain slashed down in sheets. The downpour washed Molly clean in less than a minute.

Then thunder crashed so loudly they stopped in their tracks. A flash of fire burst from the trail ahead of them. A tree, blackened and smoking, fell across the trail.

"That almost killed us!" Chelsea shouted. "We could have been crushed like bugs!"

Lightning sizzled, thunder rumbled, and rain pelted the ground. But, above the noise of the storm, the girls heard a more terrifying sound.

"*Return my treasure or die!*"

Jane whipped around and looked accusingly at Chelsea. Chelsea's arms were empty. She no longer carried the treasure.

"Don't look at me!" Chelsea whined, sounding

defensive. "Lindsay made me leave the box in the mine."

"It's true," Lindsay said. "She left the box at the entrance when we heard the second warning."

Jane looked around suspiciously. Then she remembered something.

"What about that diamond ring I saw you slip into your pocket?" she demanded. "Did you leave *that* back in the mine, too?"

The other girls, surprised, stared at Chelsea.

"What do you mean?" Chelsea said. "I have no idea what you're talking about."

Jane felt her face redden with anger. The ghost they were facing was not stupid. Somehow this ghost had known of their plans to explore the mine.

It had ripped down trail markers to lead them astray. It had stolen their water supply, and chased them through a dark mine.

Now, trees were crashing to the ground inches from where they stood.

This ghost knew a lot of things. If it believed they still had some of the treasure, they probably did.

"I know what I saw," Jane snapped. "Empty your pockets.

"No way," Chelsea said. "I know my rights, and that is an invasion of my privacy."

"Look Chelsea, our lives have been threatened," Lindsay said angrily. "Either you empty your pockets, or we'll empty them for you!"

She stepped closer to Chelsea to emphasize her point. Chelsea snorted, then reached into her pocket.

The girls watched in horror as she revealed the sapphire and diamond ring she had slipped into her pocket back in the mine.

"I can't believe you, Chelsea," Lindsay screamed. "How could you put us all in danger with your greed! You're unbelievable."

"Oh, and I guess you didn't jeopardize us all by dragging us into the mine in the first place," Chelsea shot back.

The two glared at each other.

"OK," Jane said. "We all made some mistakes." She wanted this adventure to be over.

Screaming at each other would get them nowhere.

"Now what do we do?" she asked.

"Put back my treasure or die!"

The eerie voice thundered in their ears. It sounded as if the ghost were standing right there with them.

"No way I'm going back there!" Chelsea said. "I'm not putting it back! No way!"

"Well, who else should go?" Lindsay asked. "You're the one who took it."

"Let's just all go together," Jane said. "There's safety in numbers."

So the girls started back up the trail.

Jane had never felt so wet and cold in her whole life. But at least she was alive.

As she trudged through the blinding rain, she thought of her warm bed. She thought of her room, and of her favorite doll that she still used, in private, to get to sleep. She thought of her mother.

Maybe camping wasn't her thing after all.

If she could just get through this last ordeal, she thought, everything would turn out all right.

She looked at her watch. It was 5:15. Cabin 8 was supposed to report to the flagpole by 5:30 to help prepare dinner. They would never make it back it time.

She felt herself start to cry. She wondered whether they would ever make it back at all.

Chapter Twenty-Seven

Soon, they arrived back at the top of the cliff.

Carefully, all four of them made their way over the boulder, back around the sharp crag, past the snakes and through the puddles to the entrance of the mine.

Rather than argue with Chelsea, Lindsay snatched the ring from her hand and cautiously made her way around the last bend of rock to re-enter the mine.

"I'll be right back," she said, and disappeared from view.

The other three girls stood and waited.

Then they heard a scream. Jane scrambled around the opening to help her friend.

Lindsay wasn't there.

Jane heard another scream. This one sounded

as if it was coming from below, from over the cliff.

She leaned out from the opening and looked down. What she saw took her breath away.

About five feet below where she stood, she saw Lindsay dangling in the air. She kicked her feet madly, trying to gain footing. Her hands flapped wildly, trying to grab something.

She seemed suspended in mid-air.

Then, very slowly, she began to rise as if she were floating on a cloud. She came to rest on the ground right next to Jane.

Jane grabbed her and hugged her. It was incredible, but Lindsay seemed unharmed. But there was no time for explanations now.

The girls took a deep breath and ran back to the trail.

They sprinted this time. Jane slipped and fell, but picked herself back up and continued running. Dusk had darkened the woods. She could barely see. She held her watch in front of her face. It was almost six o'clock.

She tripped on a root and fell again. Again, she

scrambled to her feet and ran on.

They shined their flashlights in front of them, trying to illuminate any obstacles. Jane didn't want to run headlong into the fallen tree.

When they reached the spot where the tree had fallen, they slowed down.

The tree was gone.

How in the world, Jane wondered, could a huge tree get struck by lightning, fall down — and then just vanish?

The girls looked at each other in horror. Then they sprinted down the trail faster than ever.

Jane saw a light ahead. She hoped it was the lights from the cabins.

But this light jumped around. It was moving — and coming toward them.

"Wait," she said. The girls huddled together and stood very still. Then they heard a voice.

"Jane, Lindsay, Molly, Chelsea!" the voice said. "Girls! Where are you?"

Jane breathed a sigh of relief. Her legs turned to jelly. It was Miss Farlie's voice!

Finally, they were safe.

<u>Chapter Twenty-Eight</u>

They charged ahead so fast they practically knocked their teacher down. All four girls began to talk at once.

"OK, OK, girls, one at a time," Miss Farlie said. "I'm sure you've had quite an adventure. I'm just glad you're all right."

She paused and looked at them. "You kids *are* all right, aren't you?"

"We're fine," replied Jane. "I think."

"Good. Now let's get you back to camp and out of those wet clothes," Miss Farlie said.

As they walked back to Cabin 8, Miss Farlie told them the cabins were all leaking. The overnight was being cut short.

"It's a good thing I found you girls," Miss Farlie said. "The buses are packed and ready to go. Hurry up and change, then come directly to the flagpole area."

Nothing had ever looked as inviting to Jane as that old rundown cabin looked right then. The girls raced inside and found puddles all over the place.

Fortunately, their clothes were in cubbies, and had stayed dry. They changed quickly, stuffed their wet things in their bags, and left Cabin 8 for good.

*   *   *

Riding home on the bus, Lindsay and Jane had a chance to talk privately.

"No one else saw you hanging there in mid-air," Jane said. "No one would believe it if we told them."

"I've never felt so weird before," Lindsay said. "It was like floating."

"How do you suppose it happened?" Jane asked.

"I guess it was the ghost's way of thanking me for putting the ring back," Lindsay said. "That ghost may have scared us, but after I fell over the cliff, it saved my life!"

"Lindsay, I was just thinking," Jane said. "If that jewelry belonged to the Armonks, and the Armonks donated the camp to the state, then the jewelry really belongs to the state, too. I'm sure it's worth a fortune. With all that money, the camp could be fixed up really nicely."

"Well I'm not going to tell anyone the treasure's there," Lindsay said. "I owe that ghost my life. If the ghost wants to keep the treasure hidden in the mine, it's OK by me!"

"I guess you're right," Jane said. "Anyway, as long as the treasure remains in the mine, there will always be an adventure waiting for the next kids who come to Camp Armonk!"